D0198718

Purchased from
Multnomah County Library
Title Wave Used Bookstore
216 NE Knott St, Portland, OR
503-988-5021

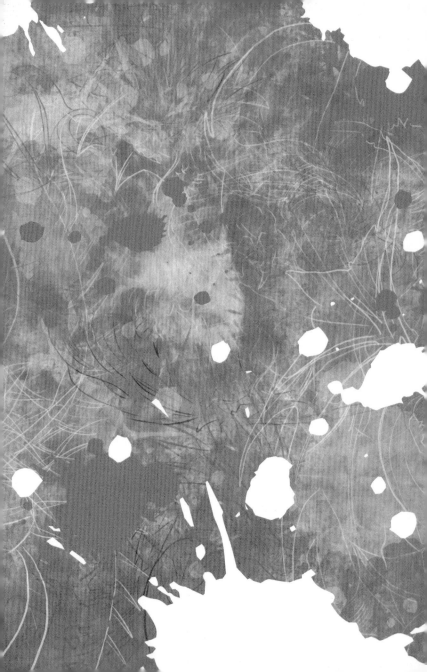

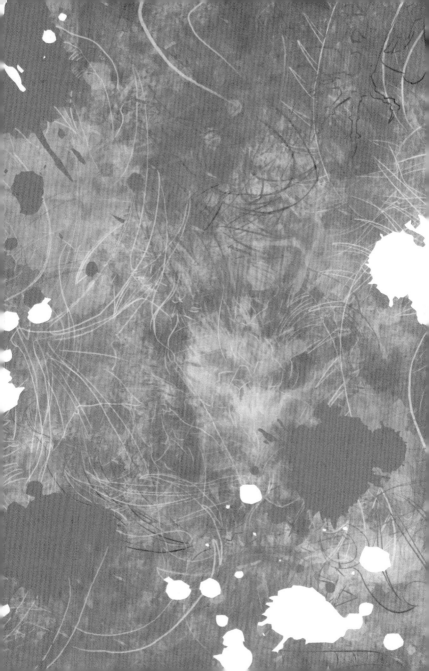

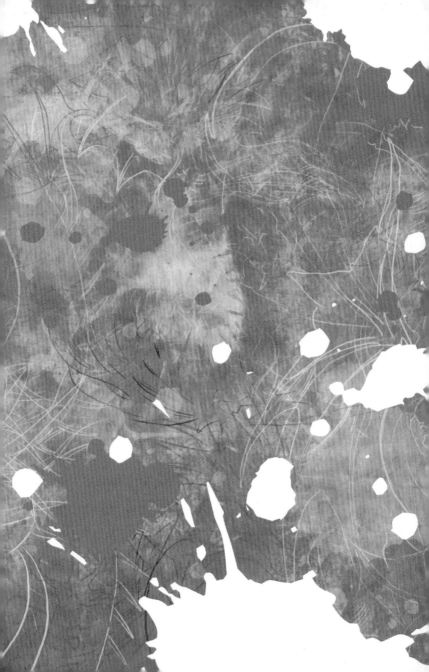

DRAGONBLOOD
TERROR BEACH

Michael Dahl

Richard Pellegrino

STONE ARCH BOOKS
www.stonearchbooks.com

Zone Books are published by
Stone Arch Books
A Capstone Imprint
1710 Roe Crest Drive
North Mankato, Minnesota 56003
www.capstonepub.com

Copyright © 2009 by Stone Arch Books

All rights reserved. No part of this publication maybe
reproduced in whole or in part, or stored in a retrieval
system, or transmitted in any form or by any means,
electronic, mechanical, photocopying, recording, or
otherwise, without written permission of the publisher.

Library of Congress Cataloging-in-Publication Data
Dahl, Michael.
    Terror Beach / by Michael Dahl; illustrated by
Richard Pellegrino.
    p. cm. — (Zone Books. Dragonblood)
    ISBN 978-1-4342-1263-4 (library binding)
    ISBN 978-1-4342-2313-5 (softcover)
    [1. Dragons—Fiction. 2. Eggs—Fiction.] I. Pellegrino,
Richard, 1980– ill. II. Title.
PZ7.D15134Te 2009
[Fic]—dc22   2008031284

Summary: The morning after a storm, Rico searches the
beach for rare and unusual objects. He doesn't believe
his eyes – the sand is covered with dozens of giant eggs.
And a strange young man is burying them. Rico and his
friend, Dr. Agon, will soon discover that the eggs are not
the key to treasure — but a doorway to terror!

Creative Director: Heather Kindseth
Graphic Designer: Brann Garvey

Printed in the United States of America.
012017
010227R

TABLE OF CONTENTS

CHAPTER 1
After the Storm 5

CHAPTER 2
The Eggs 11

CHAPTER 3
Dr. Agon 18

CHAPTER 4
Terror On the Beach 24

Introduction

A new Age of Dragons is about to begin. The **powerful** creatures will return to rule the **world** once more, but this time will be **different**. This time, they will have allies. Who will **help** them? Around the world, some young humans are making a strange **discovery**. They are learning that they were born with **dragon blood** – blood that gives them **amazing powers**.

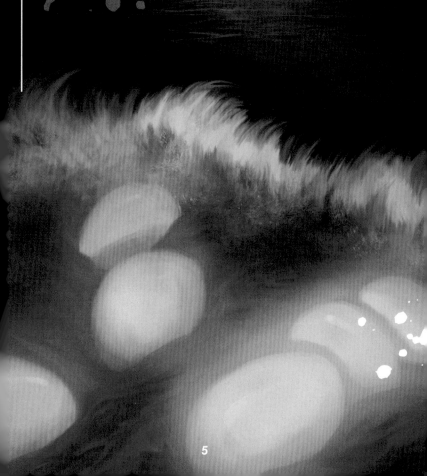

CHAPTER 1
After the Storm

A powerful **storm** hit a small island off the coast of Florida.

The next morning, Rico went down to the beach.

He was hunting for anything strange or rare.

Rico often found objects that had washed up on shore after a storm.

When he found something, Rico would take it to a scientist in town named Dr. Agon.

✦ $ $ ✦

Dr. Agon paid Rico for finding things.

That morning, Rico saw a pile of *glowing* objects lying on the sand.

They looked like giant **eggs**.

Rico also saw a young man.

The young man was **burying** the eggs in the sand.

CHAPTER 2
The Eggs

Rico hid and watched the young man.

"Why is he burying them?" wondered Rico.

He knew Dr. Agon would pay him a lot for one of those **eggs**.

When the eggs were all buried,
the young man hurried away.

Rico stepped carefully across the sand.

He picked out a spot and then began to dig with his hands.

Soon, he unburied one of the **strange eggs**.

Rico picked it up.

He felt something moving inside the egg.

Rico **yelled**. The egg tipped over in his hands.

Something inside the egg was
alive.

Rico tucked the egg under his
arm and rushed away from the
beach.

Dr. Agon would be glad to see
his new discovery.

CHAPTER 3

Dr. Agon

Rico hurried to the doctor's office.

"What did you bring me this time, Rico?" asked the doctor.

"I'm not sure," said Rico. "It was on the beach."

The doctor examined the egg
carefully.

"I think there is something inside," said Rico.

Dr. Agon felt the **SMOOTH** surface of the egg.

He had never seen anything like it before.

"There are **lots** more on the beach," said Rico.

A strange smile passed across the doctor's face. "Where are they?" he asked.

"They are buried in the sand," said Rico. "They are next to the place with all the *white* stones."

Dr. Agon pulled out a handful of money and shoved it at Rico.

Then he grabbed Rico's shoulder and shook him.

"Don't tell anyone else what you found," said the doctor.

Rico nodded his head, frightened.
Then he ran out of the office.

CHAPTER 4

Terror On the Beach

That night, a *full moon* shined down on the beach.

Dr. Agon stepped out from the shadow of some palm trees.

He was carrying a shovel.

"If there are more of those eggs," he said, "they will be worth a **fortune**."

The doctor walked across the sand.

He found the spot where Rico had dug up the first egg.

Moments later, Dr. Agon had dug up another egg.

He held it in his hands. It *glowed* in the *moonlight*.

"I'm going to be rich!" he told himself.

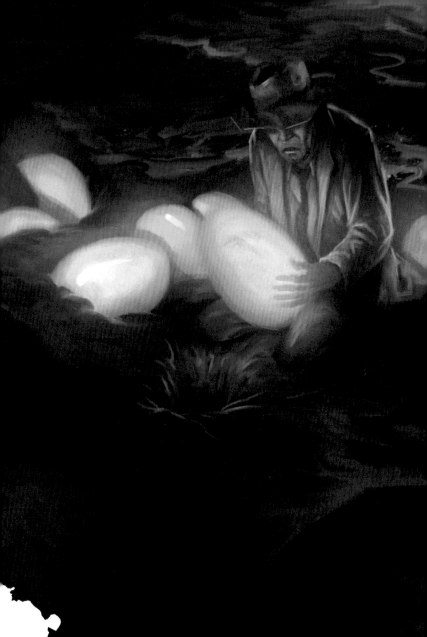

Then the shell began to move.

Tiny teeth poked through a

crack.

"Ouch!" Dr. Agon yelled and dropped the egg.

Something had  **bitten** him.

Then, all around him, the sand began to move.

Dark things began to poke out of the sand. He saw tiny **wings** and claws and sharp, little **teeth**.

Soon the beach was covered with
dark, hissing creatures.

"At last!" cried the doctor.
"I knew they were real!"

The creatures were **dragons**.

And they were hungry.

The next morning, Rico returned
to the beach.

He was hunting for more strange
objects.

All he found was a white hat.

Of Dragons and Near-Dragons

If dragons did exist and really laid eggs, they would probably lay them in the same ways their reptile cousins do. Most reptiles dig a hole in soft dirt or sand, drop their eggs into the hole, and then cover them up.

Reptiles do not produce their own body heat. They cannot sit on their eggs and keep them warm like birds do. So reptiles depend on sunlight and the warm ground to help hatch their eggs.

Female pythons sometimes curl their long bodies around a group of eggs. If it gets too cold, the pythons shiver to circulate their blood faster and warm up. This helps to warm up the eggs too.

Sea turtles return to the same beaches year after year to lay their eggs. Some sea turtles form bands of thousands of females. They climb the beaches together and lay their eggs in the middle of the night.

Reptiles can lay as many as 200 eggs at one time!

On one stretch of beach in Florida, more than 150,000 pounds of sea turtle eggs are laid each year.

Leatherback turtles travel miles through the ocean to reach their egg-laying beaches. One leatherback tracked by scientists swam more than 12,000 miles. That's more than two round-trips between Los Angeles and New York City!

ABOUT THE AUTHOR

Michael Dahl is the author of more than 200 books for children and young adults. He has won the AEP Distinguished Achievement Award three times for his nonfiction. His Finnegan Zwake mystery series was shortlisted twice by the Anthony and Agatha awards. He has also written the *Library of Doom* series. He is a featured speaker at conferences around the country on graphic novels and high-interest books for boys.

ABOUT THE ILLUSTRATOR

Richard Pellegrino is a professional illustrator who lives and works in Warwick, Rhode Island. His work has been published by CMYK, Night Shade Books, Compass Press, and Tale Bones Press. He is also an accomplished figurative painter and has shown his oil paintings in numerous galleries across the United States.

GLOSSARY

allies (AL-eyez)—people or countries that give support to each other

creature (KREE-chur)—a living thing that is human or animal

examined (eg-ZAM-uhnd)—looked carefully at something

frightened (FRITE-uhnd)—scared

rare (RAIR)—special or not common

rule (ROOL)—have power over something

surface (SUR-fiss)—the outside or outermost layer of something

terror (TER-ur)—very great fear

DISCUSSION QUESTIONS

1. Rico liked to search for treasure. Would you want to be a treasure hunter? Why or why not?

2. Was it right for Rico to take one of the eggs? Explain your answer.

3. Did you know that dragons were in the eggs? If not, what did you think was in the eggs? If so, how did you guess?

WRITING PROMPTS

1. Rico sees a young man burying the eggs on the beach. Who do you think the young man was? Write a paragraph describing him and who he works for.

2. Do you think Dr. Agon was evil or just greedy? Write a paragraph explaining your answer.

3. Were you surprised by the ending of this story? Why or why not? What do you think happened to Dr. Agon?

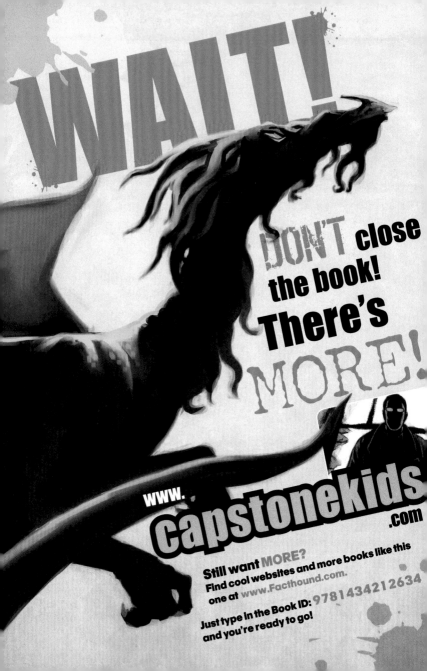

WAIT!

DON'T close the book! There's MORE!

www.capstonekids.com

Still want MORE?
Find cool websites and more books like this one at www.Facthound.com.

Just type in the Book ID: 9781434212634 and you're ready to go!